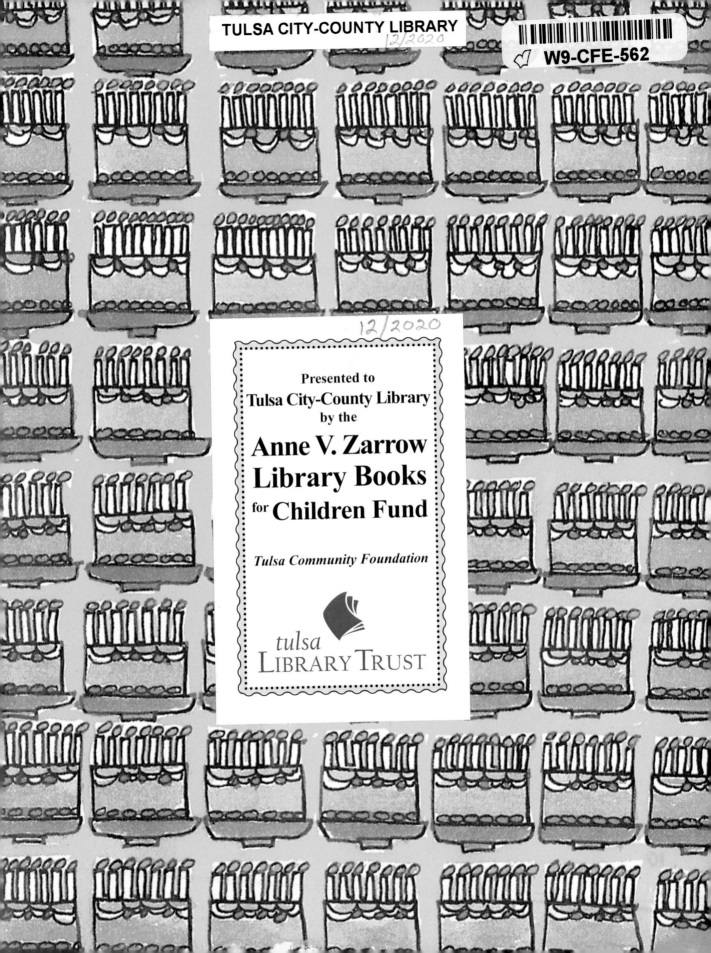

HENRY'S IMPORTANT DATE

A HENRY DUCK BOOK

ROBERT QUACKENBUSH

ALADDIN   NEW YORK LONDON TORONTO SYDNEY NEW DELHI

FOR PIET AND MARGIE,

AND NOW FOR EMMA AND AIDAN

❤ ALADDIN
An imprint of Simon & Schuster Children's Publishing Division
1230 Avenue of the Americas, New York, New York 10020
First Aladdin hardcover edition November 2020
Copyright © 1981 by Robert Quackenbush
ALADDIN and related logo are registered trademarks of Simon & Schuster, Inc.
For information about special discounts for bulk purchases, please contact
Simon & Schuster Special Sales at 1-866-506-1949 or business@simonandschuster.com.
The Simon & Schuster Speakers Bureau can bring authors to your live event. For more
information or to book an event contact the Simon & Schuster Speakers Bureau
at 1-866-248-3049 or visit our website at www.simonspeakers.com.
Book designed by Tiara Iandiorio
The illustrations for this book were rendered in watercolor, pen, and ink.
The text of this book was set in Neutraface Slab Text.
Manufactured in China 0820 SCP
10 9 8 7 6 5 4 3 2 1
Library of Congress Control Number 2019954566
ISBN 978-1-5344-1546-1 (hc)
ISBN 978-1-5344-1548-5 (eBook)

Dear Henry,
Please come to my
birthday party on Sunday.
It is from ⏰ to ⏰.
Don't be late.   Love,
                    Clara

N THE WAY TO his friend Clara's birthday party, Henry the duck got caught in traffic.

The traffic jam got worse and worse.

Henry did not want to be late,
because he had Clara's birthday
cake. The party was to start at two
o'clock.

And it was already ten minutes
to two.

At five minutes to two, Henry saw

a parking space and began parking

his car.

He thought that if he ran to a

quieter street, he would find a taxi

to take him to the party.

At exactly two o'clock, Henry's car was parked.

Then he remembered that the birthday cake was inside.

So were his keys!

He had locked the keys and the cake inside the car!

At eight minutes after two, Henry

tried to pry open a window.

The window broke!

"Stop in the name of the law!"

called a police officer.

He thought Henry was a car thief.

So Henry showed the officer his

license.

It read, HENRY THE DUCK.

The police officer let him go.

At twenty minutes after two, Henry

ran to get a taxi.

But every one was full.

When a bus came along at two thirty, Henry decided to take it.

He climbed aboard and heaved a sigh of relief.

At last, he was on his way to Clara's party.

But suddenly, at twenty minutes
to three, the motor sputtered and
then stopped.

Henry waited and waited for
the bus to go again.

Henry wondered if he would ever

get to Clara's party.

The party would be over by five

o'clock.

And it was already fifteen

minutes to three!

At three o'clock, the driver opened
the bus doors.

"Everybody off!" he said. "This
bus is out of order."

Henry went to call Clara to say
he was on his way.

But he couldn't find a phone.

At twelve minutes after three,

Henry decided that the only way

to get to Clara's was to run.

But as he went tearing down the

street, he bumped into a shopper

carrying a lot of packages.

Henry helped the shopper pick up
her packages at twenty minutes
past three.

Then he ran on with his own.

The shopper thought Henry had
one of her packages.

"Stop, thief!" she cried.

A crowd began chasing Henry and
caught up with him at twenty-five
minutes after three.

A police officer was called.

It was the same one as before.

At three thirty, Henry opened the package to show that it was his.

When the shopper saw the cake, she said she was sorry about the mistake. Once again, the police officer let Henry go.

Henry ran as fast as he could.

At ten minutes to four, Henry got

to the apartment building where

Clara lived.

   He jumped into the elevator and

pushed the button to Clara's floor.

   But halfway there, the elevator

got stuck.

Henry pushed the alarm for help.

A mechanic came to help him at four o'clock.

At four thirty, Henry was out of

the elevator.

He raced up eight floors to

Clara's apartment and rang the bell.

Clara opened the door.

"Happy birthday, Clara," said Henry.

"I'm sorry I'm late."

"Late?" asked Clara, surprised.

"But, Henry . . .

"My birthday is not until tomorrow."

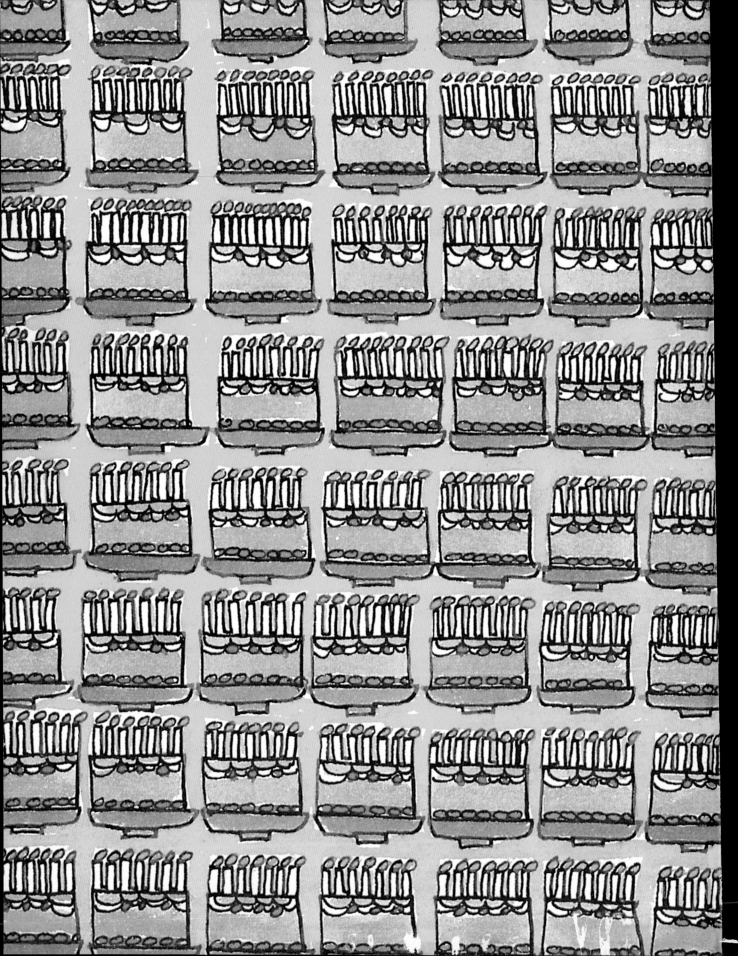